Honey Baby
Sugar Child

Honey Baby Sugar Child

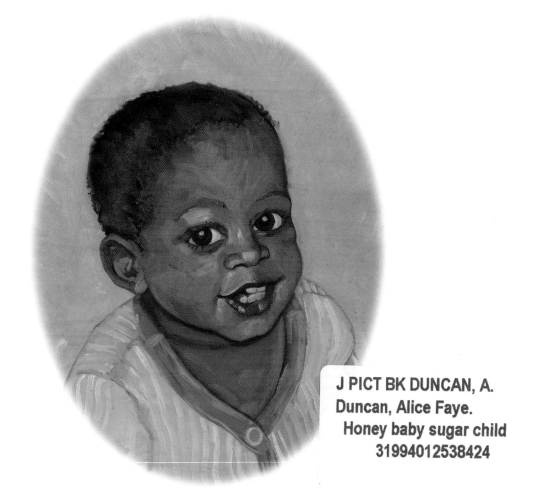

by Alice Faye Duncan
illustrated by Susan Keeter

Simon & Schuster Books for Young Readers
New York London Toronto Sydney

Honey Baby
Sugar Child,
Lord knows
I love you so.

I wanna
squeeze ya,
kiss ya,
till the sugar's gone.

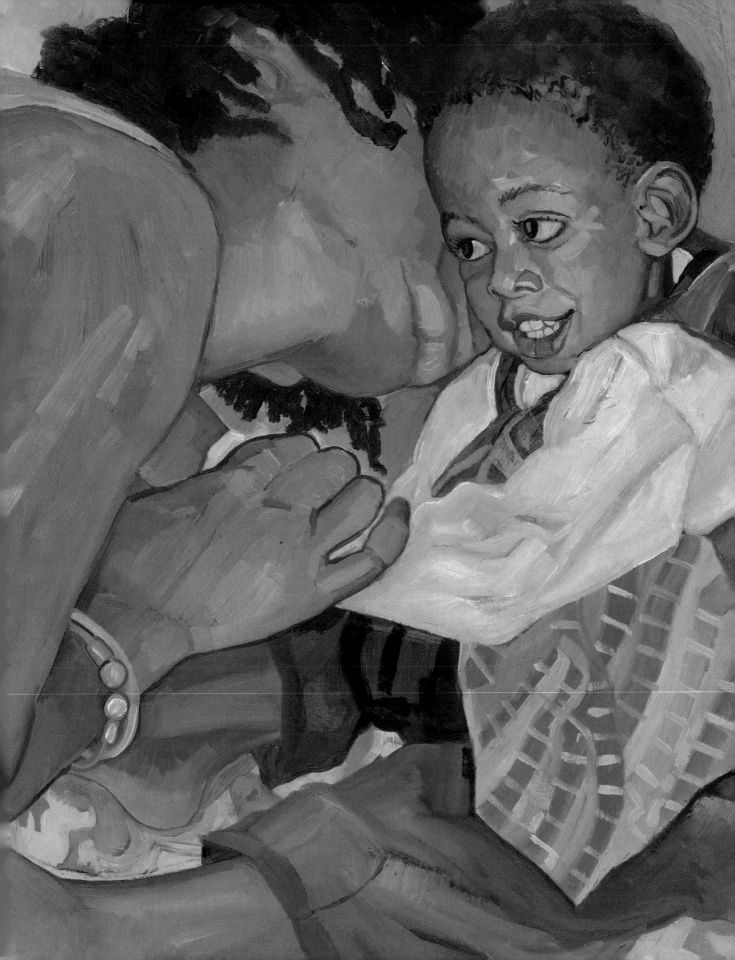

Child, I wanna
eat you up.

I wanna
hold ya,
rock ya,
swing you in my arms.

You make me wanna
dance and sing.

You make me laugh.
We jump and twirl.
We run in the green,
green grass.

And when clouds rush in
on a rainy day,
yo smile is my sunshine.

Sweet Honey Baby,
you drive me wild,
every time I see yo face.

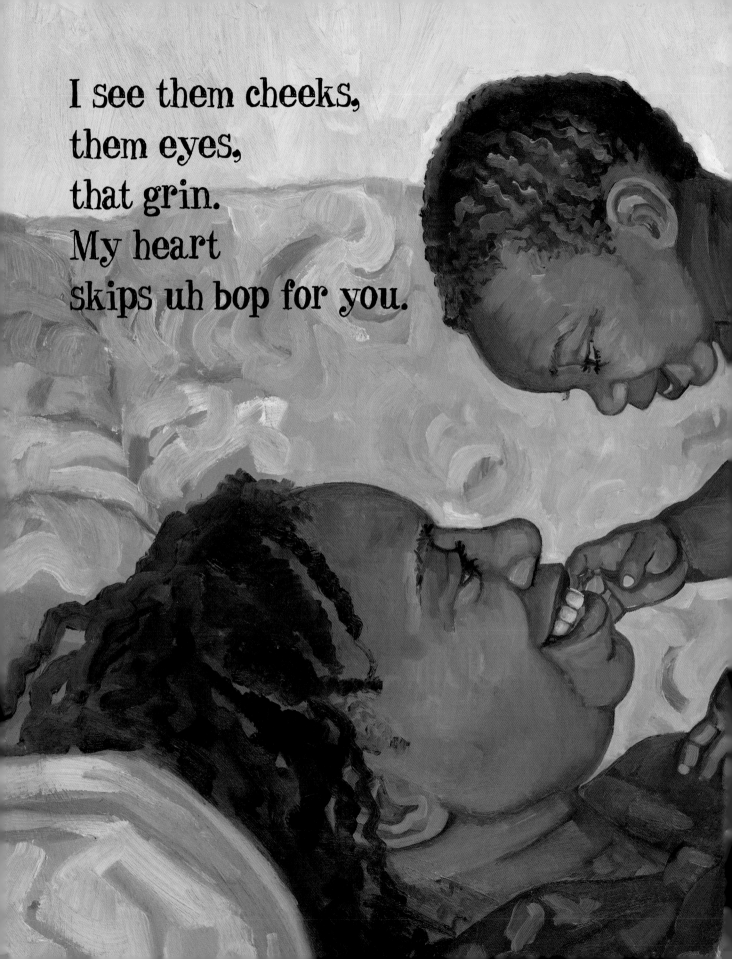

I see them cheeks,
them eyes,
that grin.
My heart
skips uh bop for you.

Sugar Child,
Sweet Puddin' 'n' Pie,
Lord knows
it's true what I say.

You my favorite patty-cake.

You the star in my crown.
You the joy in my smile.
You the angel in my dreams.

You make me laugh.
We jump and twirl.
We run in the green,
green grass.

And when clouds rush in
on a rainy day,
yo smile is my sunshine.

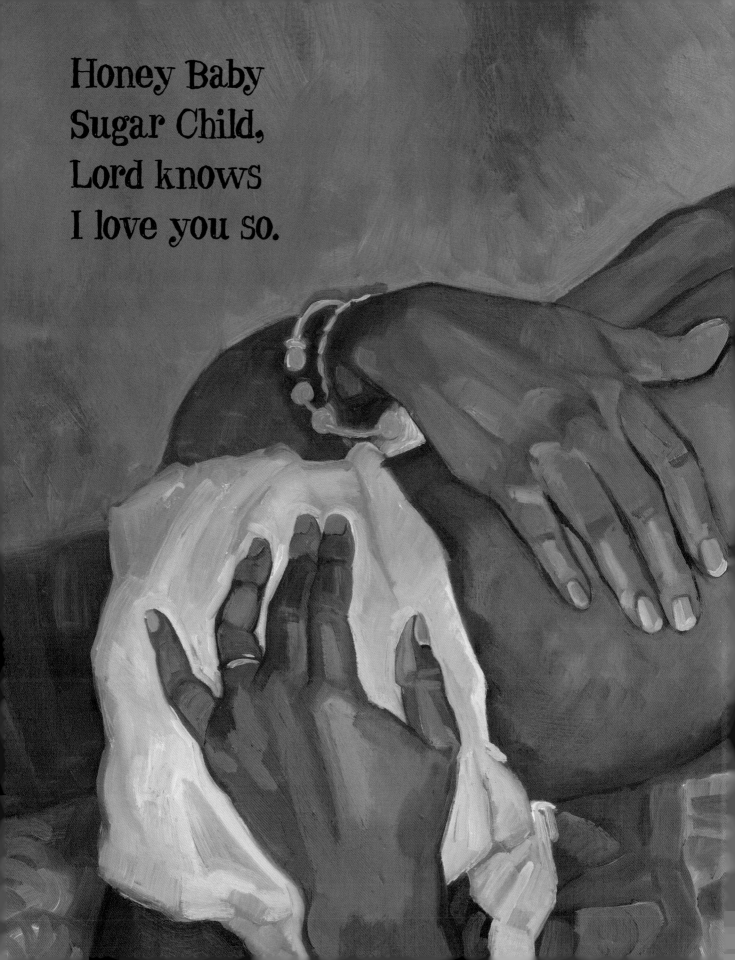

Honey Baby
Sugar Child,
Lord knows
I love you so.

And no matter how big or tall you get, and no matter how far you roam, I'm gone always be yo sweet Ma'Dear, and you gone always be my baby.

For Aunt Pat and Cousin Jessica
—A. F. D.

For Fred and Sheryl, in memory of Harriet
—S. K.

SIMON & SCHUSTER BOOKS FOR YOUNG READERS
An imprint of Simon & Schuster Children's Publishing Division
1230 Avenue of the Americas, New York, New York 10020
Text copyright © 2005 by Alice Faye Duncan
Illustrations copyright © 2005 by Susan Keeter

Book design by Lucy Ruth Cummins and Paula Winicur
The text for this book is set in Blue Century.
The illustrations for this book are rendered in oil paint on gessoed paper.

Manufactured in China
2 4 6 8 10 9 7 5 3 1

CIP data for this book is available from the Library of Congress.
ISBN 0-689-84678-9